Hairy Maclary's Rumpus at the Vet

at the

Lynley Dodd

Gareth Stevens Children's Books
MILWAUKEE

Down at the vet's
there were all kinds of pets,
with troubles and woes
from their ears to their toes.
Sniffles and snuffles
and doses of flu,
itches and stitches
and tummy ache too.
So many animals,
watchful and wary,
and Hairy Maclary
from Donaldson's Dairy.

There were miserable dogs,
cantankerous cats,
a rabbit with pimples
and rickety rats.
Mice with the sneezes,
a goat in a rage,
and Cassie the cockatoo
locked in her cage.

Cassie had claws
and a troublesome beak.
She saw something twitch
so she gave it a
TWEAK.

She pulled it so hard
that she plucked out a hair
and Hairy Maclary
jumped high in the air.

A bowl full of mice
was bundled about.
Over it went
and the mice tumbled out.

Four fussy budgies
with Grandmother Goff
flew out of their cage
when the bottom dropped off.

Grizzly MacDuff
with a bottlebrush tail
leaped out of his basket
and over the rail.

The Poppadum kittens
from Parkinson Place
squeezed through an opening
and joined in the chase.

Barnacle Beasley
forgot he was sore.
He bumbled and clattered
all over the floor.

Then Custard the Labrador,
Muffin McLay
and Noodle the poodle
decided to play.
They skidded and scampered,
they slid all around,
and bottles and boxes
came tumbling down.

What a kerfuffle,
a scramble of paws,
a tangle of bodies,
a jumble of jaws.
With squawking and yowling
and mournful meow,
they really were making
a TERRIBLE row.

Out came the vet.
"I'll fix them," she said.
But she tripped on a leash
and fell over instead.

Geezer the goat
crashed into a cage.
He butted the bars
in a thundering rage.

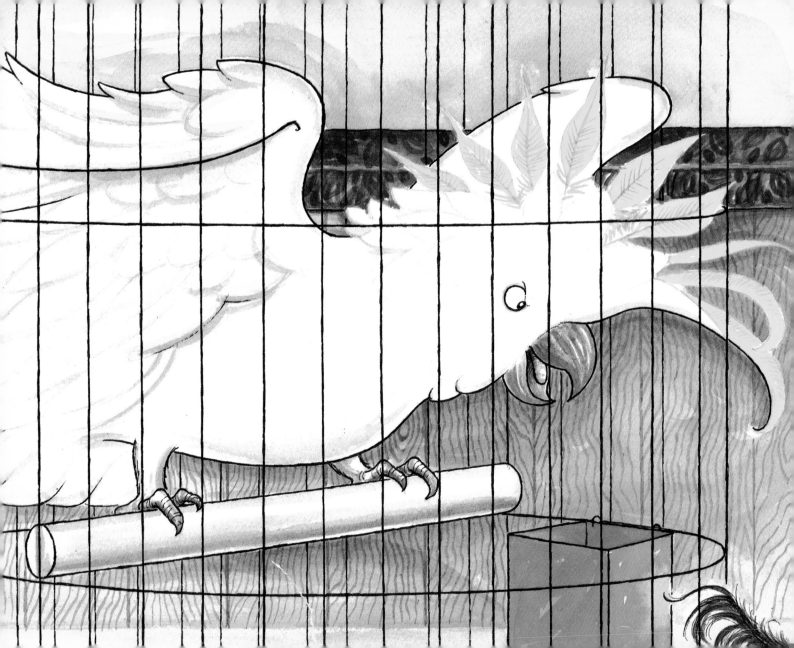

Cassie got mad.
She rattled her beak.
She saw something twitch
so she
gave
it
a . . . .

TWEAK.

Gold Star First Readers
HELP!

By Lynley Dodd . . .

THE APPLE TREE

A DRAGON IN A WAGON

HAIRY MACLARY FROM DONALDSON'S DAIRY

HAIRY MACLARY SCATTERCAT

HAIRY MACLARY'S BONE

HAIRY MACLARY'S CATERWAUL CAPER

HAIRY MACLARY'S RUMPUS AT THE VET

THE SMALLEST TURTLE

WAKE UP, BEAR

For a free color catalog describing Gareth Stevens' list of high-quality children's books, call 1-800-341-3569 (USA) or 1-800-461-9120 (Canada).

Library of Congress Cataloging-in-Publication Data

Dodd, Lynley.

Hairy Maclary's rumpus at the vet.

(Gold star first readers)

Summary: Recounts in rhyme the rumpus at the veterinarian's when all the animals get out of their cages.

[1. Animals—Fiction. 2. Veterinarians—Fiction. 3. Stories in rhyme] I. Title. II. Series.

PZ8.3.D637Hao   1990   [E]   89-43120

ISBN 0-8368-0126-1

North American edition first published in 1990 by

Gareth Stevens Children's Books

RiverCenter Building, Suite 201

1555 North RiverCenter Drive

Milwaukee, Wisconsin 53212, USA

First published in New Zealand by Mallinson Rendel Publishers Ltd. in 1989.

Text and illustrations copyright © 1989 by Lynley Dodd.

Printed in the United States of America

1 2 3 4 5 6 7 8 9 96 95 94 93 92 91 90

Gareth Stevens Children's Books
MILWAUKEE